The Gruffalo
Autumn Nature Trail

For Jesse Hall and in memory
of his big brother Skye Hall

This book belongs to

Gruffalo Explorer

....

Step inside the deep dark wood and join the
Gruffalo for a fun family nature trail.

To be a true Gruffalo Nature Explorer, you'll
need to keep your eyes open and your ears to the
ground and don't forget to take this guide with you!
It's full of games, activities and hundreds of stickers
to keep you looking for and learning about nature.

Don't forget
your wellies!

Summer is over and autumn
is here so it's time to
head outside . . .

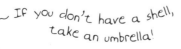 If you don't have a shell,
take an umbrella!

Signs of Autumn

Conkers

Red leaf

Yellow leaf

Squirrel

Tree stump

Feather

Bare branches

Mushroom

Acorns in cups

Blackberries

Hedgehog

Sycamore seeds

Take a stroll through the deep dark wood . . .
Look at all the pictures below. How many can you see?
Put a Gruffalo paw sticker next to each one.

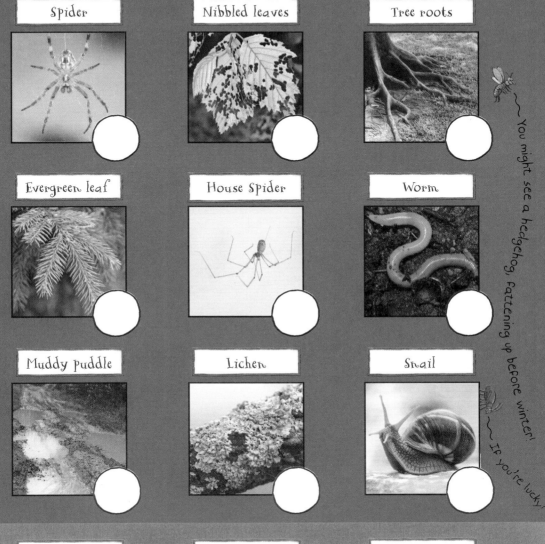

Spider

Nibbled leaves

Tree roots

Evergreen leaf

House Spider

Worm

Muddy puddle

Lichen

Snail

You might see a hedgehog, fattening up before winter! If you're lucky!

Pinecone

Conker in a shell

Dew on a spider web

EXPERT EXPLORERS

Autumn Colour

Autumn is a time when leaves change colour and fall from the trees. For every leaf you find, choose the matching colour sticker and stick it in the right box!

Bright red

Orange

Brown

Dark red

Yellow

It's hard work for a tree to keep its leaves looking good. In the autumn many trees drop their leaves so they can save energy to survive the long winter

Sticker Tree

Using your sticker page, cover this tree in autumn leaves!

Did you know?

Leaves are green because of a pigment called chlorophyll, which catches sunlight and turns it into the energy a tree needs to grow. But it takes so much energy to make chlorophyll that in winter the tree stops producing it, the green colour fades and new colours show through.

Leaf Detective

Once leaves have dropped to the floor they are easy to collect, so find as many as you can and see if you can tell what kind of tree they fell from. Use the leaf guide below to help you, then put a leaf sticker next to each one you find.

Elder	Holly	Silver Birch
Oak	Horse Chestnut	Beech
Maple	Hawthorn	Hazel

Leaf Art

Collecting leaves is great fun and there are so many things you can make with them, whether it's decorations, bunting, cards or amazing pieces of art!

Leaves can be a little damp when you pick them up, so first press them flat and leave them to dry.

You can place them between the pages of a newspaper with a weight on top and soon they'll be perfectly pretty and flat.

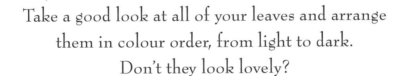

Take a good look at all of your leaves and arrange them in colour order, from light to dark.
Don't they look lovely?

Leaf Art

Just look at what else you can make
using your dried leaves and a little paint!

A fabulous fish...

Some bright bugs...

How about some leaf bunting?

You can even make some woodland hats. Simply paint some animal faces onto a long strip of card, adding eyes, nose and whiskers where needed, then glue the card into a circle and add leaves to create ears or antlers!

Fluffy feathers make perfect rabbit ears

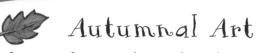

Autumnal Art

Take a look around you and see what else you can use to create some fun nature pictures. You can leave your picture on the floor for other Nature Explorers to discover.

You can use leaves, flowers, feathers, moss, twigs, stones and grass. Gather up as many different objects as you can, choose different colours and textures and see what you can create.

Transform a Leaf

Using your pencils or stickers, see what you can turn these leaves into.
A butterfly, a snail, a cheerful bird – or maybe even a dragon?

Brilliant!

That's not a leaf, it's a conker

Berry Pretty

In autumn you'll see many fruits and berries growing. They all contain the seeds of a plant, from which new plants grow. They are also an important source of food for animals and birds over the winter months. How many berries can you see? Place a special sticker by each one.

Blackberries

These grow on brambles.

Rosehips

These grow on dog rose shrubs.

Elderberries

These grow on elder trees.

As the weather gets colder and food becomes harder to find, many birds fly south to warmer countries like Africa

This is called migration!

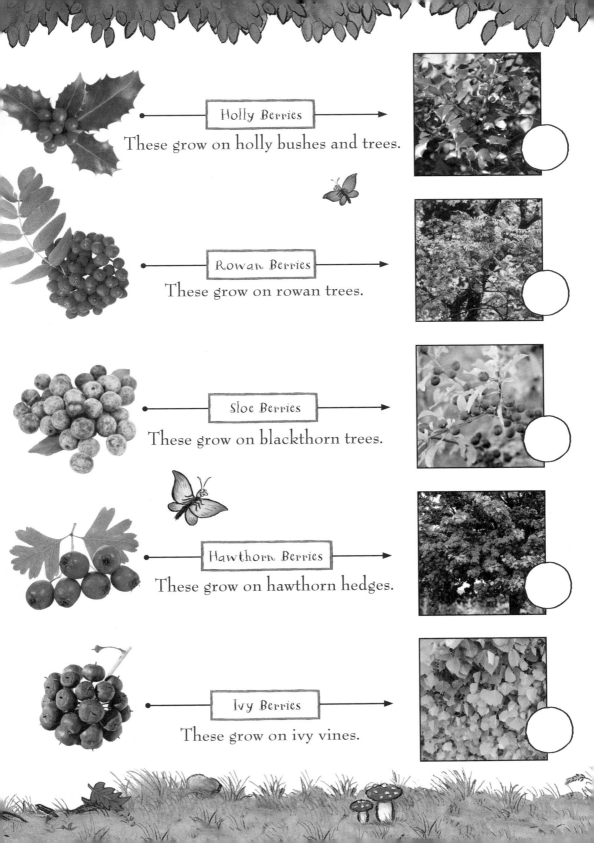

Holly Berries

These grow on holly bushes and trees.

Rowan Berries

These grow on rowan trees.

Sloe Berries

These grow on blackthorn trees.

Hawthorn Berries

These grow on hawthorn hedges.

Ivy Berries

These grow on ivy vines.

Mud Painting

You'll find mud everywhere, both dry and squelchy wet,
especially if it's been raining! So find some paper,
add some water and get creative!

You can use sticks or
brushes to paint with.
But you will get messy!

I ♥ Conkers

Conkers

Everyone loves conkers so keep your eyes peeled and see how many you can collect. If you've found some then you've also found a horse chestnut tree.

Horse chestnut trees produce flowers.

1

The flowers are pollinated by insects.

2

3

After pollination the flower develops into a shiny brown conker inside a spiky green case.

Oh, I get it

4

Later these conkers will grow into tiny little trees.

Did you know?

Conkers are poisonous for humans to eat, but squirrels and deer can eat them without feeling sick!

Nuts, Seeds and Cones

In autumn many trees produce nuts, seeds and cones.
This is a clever way for the tree to spread its seeds and from seeds new
trees can grow! Put a Gruffalo paw sticker by each seed, nut or cone you spot

Acorns

These grow on oak trees.

Conkers

These grow on horse chestnut trees.

Sycamore seeds

These grow on sycamore trees.

Why don't you find a nut and bury it?

Then come back another day
and see if you can find it!

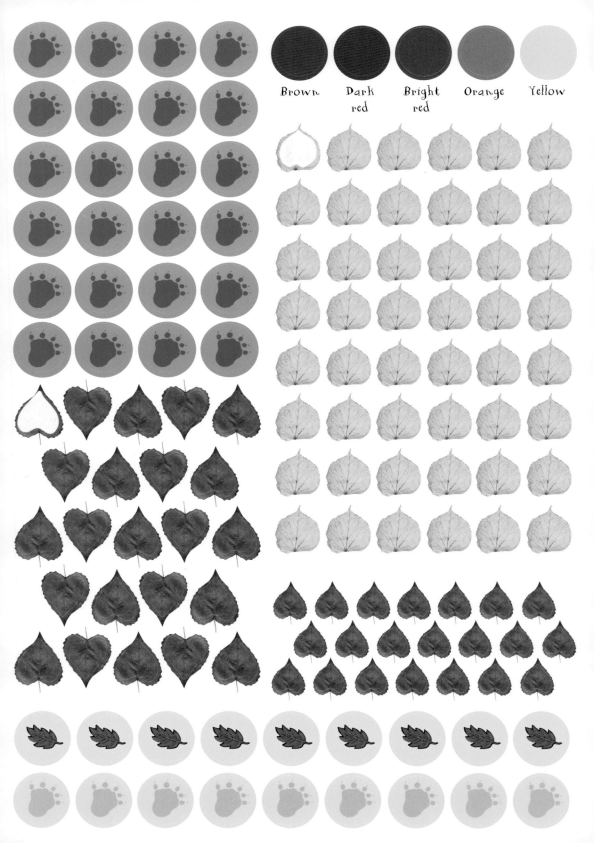

Brown · Dark red · Bright red · Orange · Yellow

I'm a Gruffalo Explorer!

I've seen a spider!

I'm a Gruffalo Explorer!

If you find a sycamore seed, drop it and watch it spin!

| Pinecones |

These grown on pine trees.

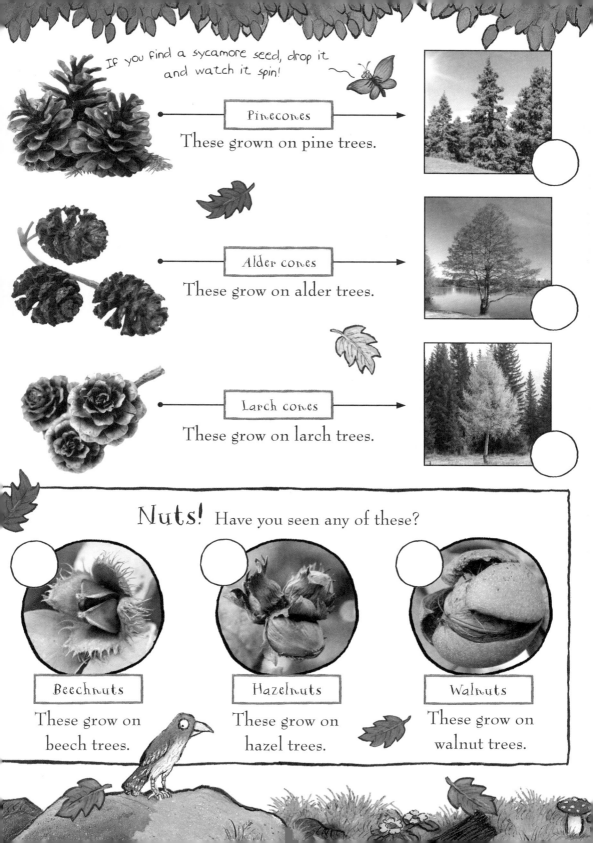

| Alder cones |

These grow on alder trees.

| Larch cones |

These grow on larch trees.

Nuts! Have you seen any of these?

| Beechnuts |

These grow on beech trees.

| Hazelnuts |

These grow on hazel trees.

| Walnuts |

These grow on walnut trees.

Cone Bird Feeder

You will need: pinecones, ribbon or string, peanut butter, a butter knife, birdseed and scissors.

When the weather gets colder it can be harder for birds to find food, so why not help by making some bird feeders? They're easy to do, they look good and they're tasty (if you're a bird).

Simply take your pinecone and tie ribbon or string to the top of the cone. With an adult to help you, carefully spread peanut butter over the cone, then sprinkle the sticky butter with birdseed and hang in the garden.

If your cone is closed, leave it in a warm place until it opens!

Did you know?
Cones grow on trees and have lots of seeds inside. When the cones open up, the seeds are released on the wind and scattered all around. From these new trees can grow.

Fungi and Mushrooms

Step into the deep dark wood and see if you can see some mushrooms and fungi. They grow all around us, up and out of the soil or on logs and trees. Put a special mushroom sticker next to each one you see.

Bracket Fungus

Common Puffball

Fly Agaric

Parasol Mushroom

King Alfred's Cake

Jelly Ear

Shaggy Ink Cap

Sulphur Tuft

The mushroom you see is the flowering part of the fungi growing under your feet

Spider Spot

When it's cold outside spiders like to
come inside to keep warm.
Have you seen a spider inside your house?
If so, give yourself a special sticker.

I've seen a spider!

Spiders have eight legs, but this poor spider is missing his.
Can you draw them?

Lift a Log, Find a Bug!

All sorts of creatures, like worms, ants, spiders and beetles, can be found under logs. See if you can find a log that's not too heavy and, with an adult to help you, lift it up and look very carefully underneath. What can you see?

Woodlouse

Millipede

Snail

Slug

Worm

Make sure you put the log carefully back in place, exactly as you found it, so the creatures underneath can get comfortable again.

Beetle

If you spot any of the insects shown above, add a bug sticker!

Travelling Seeds

From seeds new trees and plants will grow, but the seeds need to travel far and wide enough to make sure they grow a good distance away from their parents. This is called 'dispersal' and it happens in a number of different ways.

By wind

Winged seeds, like sycamore seeds, can float away on the wind.

By animal

Hungry animals and birds eat fruits and the seeds inside come out in their poo! In this way the seeds get taken to a new place where they can grow.

They arrive inside ready-made fertiliser too!

By hitch-hiking

Some seeds are covered in small hooks or hairs and so they stick to the fur of passing animals and are carried to new places.

By exploding

Some fruits explode as they ripen or if an animal brushes past them. Some seeds even have exploding pods, which means they can all scatter their own seeds!

Make a Seed Bomb!

You too can help disperse seeds and here's how:

This is another messy one. But it's fun!

You need some small seeds like grass seeds or wildflower seeds, which you mix with mud.

Add just enough water to make a fairly solid ball of mud and allow it to dry a little.

Then choose a tree and throw the seed bomb at its trunk. When it explodes the seeds will spread!

Ask an adult to help you!

By being taken away

Animals like squirrels and mice collect hazelnuts and acorns to make winter food stores, often burying them very far from the parent tree.

Explorer Chart

Fill in the explorer chart below — and don't forget
to use your weather stickers to decorate!

I went for a walk today with

. . . .

We went to

. . . .

It was

. . . .

I brought back some

. . . .

The weather was

. . . .

Design a Pumpkin

Lots of people decorate pumpkins in the autumn.
Draw some below, and decorate them with your special stickers.

~ You'll find eye, teeth and mouth stickers on the sticker page!

~ Ooh, scary!

Well done, you are now a
Gruffalo Explorer!

Reward yourself with a
special sticker like this

I'm a
Gruffalo
Explorer!

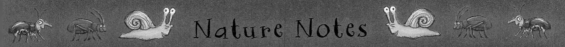

Nature Notes

Use these pages to stick in things you find, keep photos of your day or write poems or stories about the things you have seen.

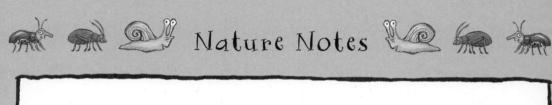

Nature Notes

Nature Notes

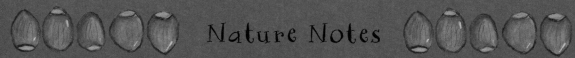